Listening to Music

Elements Age 5+

Compiled and written by Helen MacGregor

Recording produced by Stephen Chadwick

Illustrations by Alison Dexter

A & C Black · London

Contents

DURATION

Please note: tracks given in a grey box are intended for the children to listen to; tracks marked in bold in the text are primarily intended for teacher reference.

First published 1995 by A&C Black Publishers Ltd
Reprinted 1996, 2000, 2002, 2005
37 Soho Square, London, W1D 3QZ
Text © Helen MacGregor
Sound recording © A&C Black
Illustrations © Alison Dexter
Cover illustrations © Jane Tattersfield
Edited by Sheena Roberts
Sound engineering by Stephen Chadwick
Printed in Great Britain by St Edmundsbury Press

A&C Black uses paper produced with elemental chlorine-free pulp, harvested from managed sustainable forests.

Visit our website: www.acblack.com

DYNAMICS

TEMPO

TIMBRE

What you need to know, *30*   Listening links, *30*

TEXTURE

What you need to know, *38* Listening links, *38*

PITCH

What you need to know, *46*   Listening links, *46*

STRUCTURE

What you need to know, *58*   Listening links, *58*

DURATION

What you need to know about duration

Music is made up of sounds and silences of different lengths. They may be regulated by pulse and beat. Groupings of sounds and silences make rhythm. All these are aspects of duration.

The length of sounds

All sounds last for different lengths of time: humming with the voice can last several seconds until the singer needs to take another breath; a single clap makes a very short sound. Many instruments can be played in a variety of ways to produce different lengths of sound: a suspended cymbal tapped with a beater makes a clash which gradually dies away; a cymbal held by its edge while tapped makes a very short sound (see Investigations 1 and 2).

Pulse and beat

A lot of music, but not all, is based on a regular underlying pulse - like the steady tap of walking feet. As **track 1** shows, pulse can be at different speeds.

The pulse of a piece of music is grouped in twos to give it a marching beat: **1** 2 **1** 2 **1** 2 - like the **L** R **L** R of marching feet. It is grouped in threes to give it a waltz beat: **1** 2 3 **1** 2 3. Listen to **track 2** to hear this effect. A pulse can also be grouped in fours, or fives, or sixes, and so on.

Rhythm

Combinations of short sounds, long sounds and silences make rhythms, as **track 3** demonstrates.

In **Mu min xin ge** the children will be able to hear duration used in two very different ways. In the first section there is no regular pulse and the Chinese flute and dulcimer play long sounds. The second section has a fast regular pulse with rhythms made up of many short sounds.

In **African Drum** the children will hear how the rhythms of speech relate to rhythms played on a drum.

Listening links with classroom music

Classroom percussion instruments are made of a variety of materials which produce different lengths of sound when they are struck once with a beater. The metal bar of a glockenspiel will ring for several seconds longer than the wooden bar of a xylophone.

Investigation 1

Choose a selection of classroom percussion instruments and let groups of children investigate the length of the sound each makes when struck once with a beater.

Give each group a stopwatch to time the sounds. This will give approximate figures for comparison (individual children will hear each sound differently - one may be further away from the instrument than another, but they should be able to reach agreement with general comparisons.)

Record the results on a simple graph. What do the children notice about the relationship between the length of sound and the material the instrument is made of?

Here is a sample graph:

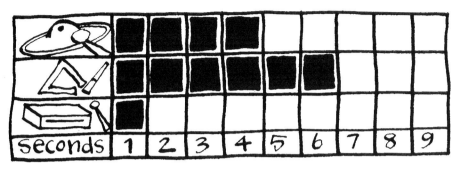

Investigation 2

The children can now discover new ways of playing the same instruments to produce long sounds on all those which previously made short sounds, and short sounds on those which previously made long sounds.

Encourage them to find their own methods. Here are some:

long first time - short second time

- hold a metal instrument while playing it to prevent it from vibrating freely
- strike once then quickly put your hand on the instrument

short first time - long second time

- use two beaters to play a 'roll' alternating hands, LRLR
- wiggle a beater around inside a hollow woodblock
- scrape the skin of a drum with a fingertip
- roll a marble inside a tambour

Listening links with the other tracks

After the activities on **Mu min xin ge** and **African drum**:

Compare track 22 Aquarium with track 26 Fossils

In *Aquarium*, notice the long slides on the glockenspiel and the long notes of the melody played by the violin.

In *Fossils*, short sounds are created by the hard wooden beaters playing on the wooden bars of the xylophone, by the short, sharp clusters of sound played on the piano, and by plucking the strings of the violins, violas, cellos and double basses (the stringed instruments of the orchestra).

Listen to track 11 March past of the kitchen utensils

As in all marches the pulse is grouped in twos like marching feet. As you listen, ask the children to count the pulse and mark the beat by tapping fingers on palms on 1 and shaking their fingers in the air on 2:

Say:

	1	2	1	2	1	2
	tap	*shake*	*tap*	*shake*	*tap*	*shake*

Listen to track 44 Divisions on a ground

This has a pulse which is grouped in threes. Listen with the children, count the pulse and mark the beat by tapping fingers on palms on 1, and shaking fingers on 2 and 3:

Say:

And	1	2	3	1	2	3	1
	tap	*shake*	*shake*	*tap*	*shake*	*shake*	*tap*

Can the children find other action patterns to do while listening to the music?

long • short • pulse • rhythm • beat • silence

5

Mu min xin ge

This piece of music (pronounced moo min hsin gay) is an instrumental version of a traditional Chinese song about a Mongolian cattleman. Two of the instruments you will hear are the Chinese bamboo flute, and the yang quin (pronounced yang chin), a stringed instrument which is played by striking its strings with two bamboo beaters:

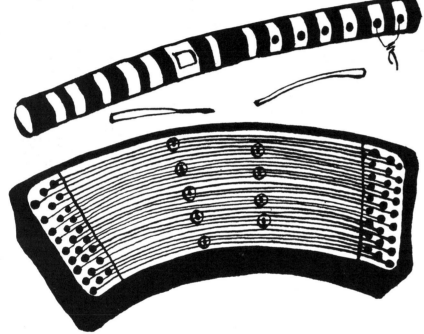

In the first section the instruments play long sounds: the flute player has to take deep breaths to control the sound, and the yang quin player beats the strings very quickly, RLRLRL, which keeps them vibrating.

The second section describes the cattleman galloping on his horse and rounding up his cattle (but don't reveal this to the children yet). The instruments are played in a different way. This time they make very short sounds which give the impression of speed and movement.

Activity 1

Crocodile snap

What you will need
- enlarged photocopies of the cards opposite.

In this game the children make layers of long animal sounds using their voices. When they hear a short sound, the crocodile snap, they must stop or the crocodile will catch them! Before the game, set the crocodile card aside and show the children the other cards one by one. Ask them to make the appropriate animal sound with their voices, sustaining it until you change to the next card.

Questions you might ask
All these animals make different sounds, but the sounds are the same in one way. Can you say how? (They are all long.)

Now show the children the crocodile snap card and ask them what sound they could make for this - they may suggest snapping hands together, clashing teeth, saying 'snap'.

Questions you might ask
Does the crocodile make a long sound or a short sound when it snaps its teeth together? (Short.)
How is this different from the other animal sounds we made? (They were long sounds.)

To play the game shuffle all the cards. Show the first card to one child. This child will make the animal sound to match the card and keep repeating it. Now show the second card to another child. This child will add this second animal sound over the first. Continue like this until one of the children goes 'SNAP' on seeing the crocodile card.

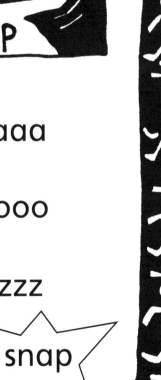

 baaaaaaaaaaaaaaaaaaaaaaaaaaaaaaaaaaaaaa

 mooooooooooooooooooooooooo

 bzzzzzzzzzzzzzzzz

 snap

Mu min xin ge

Activity 2

Sounds in space

In this game the children will use their voices to investigate long and short sounds of their own choice, creating a sound picture describing a journey through space.

Explain to the children that you are all in a space ship travelling through the galaxies. All that you can hear are the sounds of the computers and machines on board the space ship. Ask the children to take a breath and then very gently make a long sound, each child choosing their own computer or machine sound and keeping it the same once they have started. They should each take a quick breath whenever they need one.

You say: 'Breathe and -'

    Child 1   mmmmmmmmmmmmmmmmmmmmmmmmmmmmmmmm
    Child 2   zzzzzzzzzzzzzzzzzzzzzzzzzzzzzzzzzzzzzzzz
    Child 3   woooooooooooooooooooooooooooooooooooo
    Child 4   aaaaaaaaaaaaaaaaaaaaaaaaaaaaaaaaaaaaaaaa
    Child 5   etc

Encourage the children to listen to the results. Are all the sounds they are making different?

Now explain that sometimes the space ship comes to a meteor storm and has to travel through small, rocky pieces of stars and meteors. Ask the children to suggest sounds they can make with their voices to represent the rocks hitting the outside of the space ship at random.

Questions you might ask
When the rocks hit the space ship do you think they make long or short sounds? (Mostly short, but some children may say that the metal case of the space ship will ring.)

You may like the children to listen to the sound of a computer when it is turned on, and compare it with a pebble tapping a metal container.

Ask the children to choose a short meteor sound to make when you give the signal. You say: 'Meteor storm' -

    Child 1 plik plik   plik plik plik   plik   plik
    Child 2   tip tiptip   tiptiptiptip   tiptip
    Child 3 t   t   ttttt   t t   ttttttttttttttttttttt
    Child 4   ckck   ckck ck ckckckckck   ck
    Child 5 etc

Say 'All clear', when you want the children to stop.

Now choose a captain for the space ship. The captain will call out the signals for the other children to make long computer sounds or short meteor sounds:

    'All systems go'   long sounds
    'Meteor storm'   short sounds
    'All clear'   long sounds
    'Mission over'   stop

To start the game the captain must say 'All systems go', but the space ship may travel through several meteor storms before 'Mission over'.

Extension 1

What you will need
- a small selection of percussion instruments.

Play the game with sound signals. This time the captain chooses two instruments - one which makes a long sound, the other a short sound. The long sound signals to the rest of the children to make long computer sounds with their voices. The short sound signals a meteor storm.

Play the game in small groups or 'crews', so that everyone can have a turn at being captain. Each captain should find a new way of playing a long and a short signal. (**Track 4** and the picture below demonstrate *Sounds in space*.)

mmmmmmmmmmm plik plik plikplikplik mmmmmm
zzzzzzzzzzzzzz tip tiptip tip zzzzzzz
Wooooooooooooooo t t t t t Wooooooo
aaaaaaaaaaaaaaaa ckck ckck ckckck ck aaaaaaaa

Listen to track 5 Mu min xin ge

Questions you might ask
In the first part of the music did you hear mostly long sounds or mostly short sounds? (Mostly long.)
Did you recognise any of the instruments you heard? (Flute and stringed instruments.)
How do you think the flute player made the long sounds? (By taking deep breaths and blowing for a long time on each note.)
How is this similar to the way we made long sounds with our voices? (We also took breaths to make the sound last.)
In the second part, are the sounds in the music mostly short or mostly long? (Short.)

Does the second part of the music with its short sounds seem different from the first part with its long sounds? How? (It seems faster, livelier, happier.)

Music does not always describe a scene or story, but you may find after listening to this piece that the children want to share what they think the music is describing. Collect these ideas together and discuss them before you reveal the theme of the Chinese song. The children will often have valid reasons for their ideas and be able to make links with other music they have heard.

When you have told the children about the galloping cattleman in the second section of the music, ask them what they think the slow section might be describing.

African drum

This piece is played on a dondo (pronounced don-**doe**), a double-headed drum from West Africa. The drum is held under one arm and played with a wooden stick. Strings linking the two drum skins can be squeezed by the player. By stretching the drum skins tighter in this way, the drum is made to play higher sounds. These drums can 'talk' by copying the long and short sounds and the up and down sounds of speech.

Activity 1

I want some peanuts

In this activity the children start by investigating rhythm with their voices by learning how speech makes patterns of long and short sounds. They will hear how the music of an African drum can imitate these rhythms of speech. By learning how to play with word rhythms, they can then go on to make up their own rhythm patterns on a drum.

Teach these four lines of words to the children by saying a line and letting them repeat it after you. Repeat each line as many times as you like.

Say the words as you would in normal speech - there is no regulating pulse.

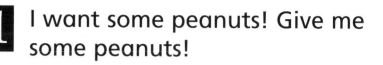

1 I want some peanuts! Give me some peanuts!

2 Did you say please? I'll give you some if you say please.

3 Chocolate on my fingers, peanuts in my pocket!

4 Gobbly gobbly gobbly, lubbly jubbly. Eat it up, yeah!

Now say the words in a different voice, e.g.

Loud, demanding voice:

> I **want** some peanuts. **Give** me some peanuts!

Whining, pleading voice:

> I want some **pea___**nuts. Give me some **pea___**nuts.

Ask individual children to think of a way to say one of the lines for the others to copy. (It may help the children answer the questions below if you record and play back the suggestions.)

Questions you might ask
Did (child's name) make any long sounds? Which words were long?
Did (child's name) make any short sounds? Which words were short?

Listen to track 6 African drum

The four drum rhythms fit the four lines of words of *I want some peanuts*. Rhythms 1, 2 and 3 are played four times each, rhythm 4 is played once.

Questions you might ask
What did you notice about the music you heard? (It was a drum, it was talking, it was playing what we were saying.)
Did the drum say the word rhythms in the same way or differently from ours? (Some words or whole phrases may have been the same as the children's suggestions.)

Here is another set of words which the drum might have been saying (you can hear it on **track 7**). It is a conversation. Divide the class into two groups - Group 1 say rhythms 1, 3 and 4, Group 2 answer with rhythm 2. Afterwards, swap parts.

1 I like banana,
yellow banana.

2 D'you want it peeled? I think you'd better have it peeled.

3 Why did you give me this squashy, ripe banana?

4 Yucky yucky yucky, squishy squishy. Won't eat this. No!

Extension

What you will need
- space for the children to sit in a circle
- a small hand drum or tambour

This game gives individual children the opportunity to say a word or simple phrase in a rhythm of their own choice, and later to play the rhythm on a small drum.

Sit the children in a circle and choose a question, e.g 'What's your favourite food?' Everyone in the circle will say the question together, pausing afterwards for each child to answer in turn, saying their favourite food in any way they like with *no time limit or regular pulse to fit the answer into.*

Questions you might ask
Which favourite food made a long sound (or sounds)?
Which made a short sound (or sounds)?
Which favourite food was made up of both long and short sounds?

Play the game again, this time passing the drum round the circle. Each person now takes a turn at playing the rhythm of their favourite food on the drum instead of saying it. Again there should be no pressure to keep to a pulse. Some children will need help transferring all the syllables of their favourite foods onto the drum (listen to **track 8**).

All	Solo	All	Solo
what's your favourite food?	macaroni cheese with green peas	what's your favourite food?	chips and egg and chocolate ice cream

Play the game with other simple questions.

DYNAMICS

loud • quiet • getting louder • getting quieter

What you need to know about dynamics

Dynamics in music means volume - degrees of loud and quiet. When they write out their music, composers often include dynamic markings to indicate to the performers how the volume should change.

Traditionally, Italian terms are used to describe dynamics, but modern music often includes instructions in the language of the composer.

There can be a big contrast between the volume of outdoor and indoor music. The suggestions in *Listening links* below will help you explore this aspect. Dynamic contrasts within a piece of music are explored in the activities on **March past of the kitchen utensils** and **Alpha**. In the former, the composer uses mainly quiet dynamics, but there are sudden, loud bursts of sound, which give the listener a surprise. In **Alpha** the music begins very quietly and builds gradually towards a loud, exciting climax.

Here are some Italian terms for dynamics:

piano (pi-**ah**-no)	*p*	quiet
mezzo-forte (**met**-zo **for**-tay)	*mf*	medium loud
forte (**for**-tay)	*f*	loud
crescendo (cre-**shen**-do)	<	gradually getting louder
diminuendo (di-**mi**-new-**en**-do)	>	gradually getting quieter

Listening links with classroom music

Many modern day musical instruments would at one time have been intended either for outdoor or indoor playing. Instruments used for processions and outdoor celebrations need to make a sound loud enough to carry to a large audience in the open air. Trumpets, drums, and cymbals are all typical outdoor instruments. Instruments played for social occasions in the home with a small closely gathered audience can be more delicate in sound, e.g. flute, violin, folk guitar.

Ask the children to choose some loud instruments to play as you all sing *The grand old Duke of York*. Sing and play it in a procession round the school playground. Ask the whole school to come and listen. Encourage the children to think about the suitability of the instruments they have chosen. Will they be loud enough? Can they be easily carried?

Choose an indoor song like *Polly put the kettle on* to sing and play to another class. When the children are selecting their instruments they will need to consider the volume again so that the music can be heard clearly within the room, but will not disturb other classes.

With the children in pairs, ask each child to make a solo piece to play to their partner. They will sit facing one another to listen. How loud does their instrument need to be this time?

Listening links with the other tracks

Ask the children to consider which of these two pieces of music would be heard more clearly outside.

Listen to track 44 Divisions on a ground

(This is typical indoor music to be played amongst friends or to a small audience.)

Listen to track 18 Raghupati Rāghava Rājaram

(This is outdoor religious festival music used during processions from house to house.)

March past of the kitchen utensils

Composer: Ralph Vaughan Williams, born Surrey, 1872-1958. Vaughan Williams had decided he wanted to be a composer by the age of nine and went on to study composition for many years. He wrote *March past of the kitchen utensils* as part of a student production at Cambridge and, like Haydn in his *Surprise Symphony*, he uses loud, unexpected bursts of sound to wake up and amuse the audience!

Activity 1

Hunt the spoon

What you will need
- a wooden spoon

The object of this game is to work as a team to lead the way to a spoon hidden in the classroom using aural signals: loud for hot, quiet for cold.

Choose one child to leave the room. Hide the spoon, making sure everyone in the class sees the hiding place. Everyone will help to lead the chosen child to the spoon by clapping more loudly as he or she moves nearer to the hiding place, and clapping more quietly as he or she moves away.

March of the wooden spoons

What you will need
- three wooden spoons: small, medium and large (use real spoons, or enlarged photocopies of the pictures above)

Three wooden spoons march around the kitchen in turn and show the children the difference between quiet, in-between, and loud.

Show the children how each wooden spoon walks around the kitchen ('walk' it in the air or tap it on your knee). Each spoon should walk at the same steady pace.

Ask the children to clap their hands in time to the spoons as they move (stopping when they stop).

Questions you might ask
What is different about the three spoons? (Their sizes - small, medium, large.)
How can we show by the way we clap that they are different sizes? (By clapping at three different volumes, e.g. tap one finger on palm for quiet, tap four fingers on palm for in-between, and clap hands for loud.)

Let individual children conduct using the spoons.

Crash

March past of the kitchen utensils

Extension

What you will need
- a set of three spoons for each group

Make an opportunity for small groups of children to play the spoons game. Make sure everyone has a turn at conducting with the spoons. Encourage the children to discuss the results and play to other groups.

Activity 2

Midnight in the kitchen

What you will need
- untuned percussion instruments such as small drums, tambourines, woodblocks

It is midnight and while everyone is asleep, the kitchen tools, which have worked hard preparing food all day, creep out to have fun. They try their best not to wake anyone up.

Teach the children the chant, *Midnight in the kitchen* (**Track 9**). Keep a steady pulse (marked by the mouse) as you say the words in a whisper, and ask the children to walk two fingers on the palm of the other hand as they say the words.

Choose a few children to tap some of the percussion instruments on the pulse as you say the chant together again.

Questions you might ask
Were the instruments quiet enough for us to hear the words?
Can you think of other ways of making quiet sounds using the same instruments? (E.g. tap with a fingernail, touch one jingle on the tambourine, put the instrument on the floor to muffle the sound.)

Divide the children into small groups and let them experiment with the instruments, finding the quietest ways of playing them with the chant. Let each group show their ideas to the rest of the children.

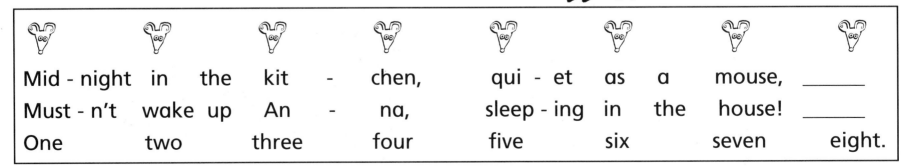

Mid - night	in	the	kit	-	chen,	qui - et	as	a	mouse,	_____
Must - n't	wake	up	An	-	na,	sleep - ing	in	the	house!	_____
One		two	three		four	five	six		seven	eight.

Extension 1

What you will need
- a collection of kitchen utensils (nothing sharp!), e.g.

In small groups, let the children explore ways they can find to play their kitchen sound-makers quietly as they say *Midnight in the kitchen* again.

Extension 2

What you will need (as above)

Now explain to the whole class that this time, as the kitchen tools creep around the kitchen, they forget to be quiet just once. Try this first. Choose a number from 1 to 8. Count together quietly, then clap once very loudly on the chosen number:

1   2   3   4   5   ⭐6   7   8

Discuss hand signals the children might use to indicate quiet and loud. Choose a conductor to give the signals. Before beginning, the conductor must tell everyone which number he or she has chosen to be loud. The aim is to play or clap as quietly as possible on all of the counts except the chosen number, which should be very loud to create a contrast. This may require some practice.

Questions you might ask
Did we all manage to play or clap loudly on the same number? (If not) what would help us? (Counting individually, watching the conductor, listening, concentrating.)

If we played this to someone who didn't know that we were going to play loudly on one number, how do you think they would feel? (They might be surprised, jump out of their skin, get a shock, think it's funny.)

Extension 3

What you will need
- space to sit in a circle

Choose one child to sit in the middle of the circle pretending to be asleep. Choose a number from 1 to 8, and make sure everyone (except the child in the middle) knows what it is. Everyone chants *Midnight in the kitchen* together and quietly taps the pulse on their palm with one finger. On the chosen number everyone claps one loud clap to wake up the sleeper. If the child in the centre can work out which number was chosen, they choose someone else to go to sleep. If not they have another go. Try the game with kitchen instruments.

Extension 4

What you will need (as in extension 1)

Encourage the children to make up group pieces of music describing the kitchen tools coming out at midnight. They can draw picture scores showing which tools forget to be quiet.

March past of the kitchen utensils

Listen to track 10 Number quiz

You will hear three number patterns. In each, one number is played loudly. As you listen count 1 to 8 very quietly with the children. (There are four clicks before the count begins.)

1 2 3 4 5 6 7 8
1 2 3 4 5 6 7 8
1 2 3 4 5 6 7 8

Questions you might ask
Was the music mostly loud or quiet? (Quiet.)
Which number were we on when the instruments played loudly? (First example: 4; second: 8; third: 3.)

Listen to track 11 March past of the kitchen utensils

Questions you might ask
Was the music we listened to mostly loud or mostly quiet? (Mostly quiet with loud bursts of sound.)
Was the last sound you heard loud or quiet? (Loud.)

For the next activity, you need to be able to count from 1 to 8 while the children listen to *March past of the kitchen utensils*. **Track 12** demonstrates how to do this.

Listen to track 11 again

Count with the children - 1 2 3 4 5 6 7 8 (keep repeating.) Can you find out on which numbers the loud sounds are played? (Alternately on 7 and 8.)

Alpha

Composer: Vangelis is a composer who writes music for films using computers and electronics. *Alpha* begins with a very quiet crackling sound; perhaps something hatching out of an egg? After this introduction we hear a very simple melody repeated over and over again. As the music progresses, Vangelis adds more instruments, which increase the volume and change the mood from calm to thrilling.

Activity 1

Alpha dance

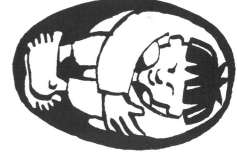

What you will need
- a large space (a hall)

In this activity the children perform a simple dance as they listen to the music. They will be following instructions from you, so you will need to make yourself familiar with the music and the movements for the dance shown opposite. **Track 13** will help you to hear how the movements fit the music.

To perform the dance, the children will need to find a clear space and curl up as small as possible as if they were inside an egg. When they hear the egg beginning to crack open they will start to stretch their fingers to break the eggshell. As the music plays, they gradually stretch parts of their bodies and grow until they are free to move around the large space.

Listen to track 14 Alpha

The children move to your instructions as they listen. (See movement instructions opposite. Questions on page 18.)

Alpha dance

(COUNT)	4	1	2	3	4	1	2	3

Repeat each line of actions four times

SAY

One hand stretch	and	curl
other hand stretch	and	curl
one foot stretch	and	curl
other foot stretch	and	curl
one arm stretch	and	curl
other arm stretch	and	curl
one leg stretch	and	curl
other leg stretch	and	curl
kneel and stretch	and	curl
both arms stretch	and	curl
stand and stretch	and	curl
legs and stretch	and	curl
step out and stretch	and	curl
move round and stretch	and	curl

Repeat to end

17

Alpha

Track 14 Alpha (continued)

Questions you might ask
Which parts of your body were moving when the music was quietest? (Fingers and toes.)
What did you notice about the music when I asked you to stretch your arms? (The music was louder, the drum started playing.)
Which instrument joined in when I asked you to stretch your legs? (The trumpet.)
Did the music stay loud or become quiet at the end? (It stayed loud.)

Play track 14 again

Encourage the children to choose their own movements which grow larger and larger, using the music as a signal. Ask the children to suggest other ways of showing how the music gets louder by the way they move. They may choose to start with a small group dancing, joined by others as they hear more instruments at the beginning of each section.

Activity 2

Pass it on

What you will need
- a large space (a hall)

Stand the children in a long line and explain that you are going to pass an action along the line to the person at the front. You will stand at the back of the line and tap lightly (and keep on tapping) on the shoulder of the person in front, who then starts to tap the next child's shoulder. In this way the action should pass along the line until everyone is tapping. When the last person has joined in the action stops.

Try this with different actions, e.g. touching elbows, holding waists, patting backs. Now form the line into a circle and pass an action round it. Remind the children to keep doing the action after they have passed it on. When the last person has joined in the action stops.

Extension 1

What you will need
- space to sit in a circle (facing inwards)

Play *Pass it on* with sounds instead of actions, e.g.

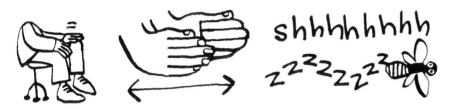

shhhhhhhh

zzᶻᶻzzzzᶻ

Before beginning make sure the children understand these rules:

- they must not join in until the sound is passed on by a neighbour (some children will tend to join in as soon as they *hear* the message, and play out of turn);
- they must keep making the sound once they have joined in;
- when everyone has joined in, they must stop one by one (you may have to help the children stop one after the other by pointing to each in turn).

Questions you might ask
What happened to the sound as it travelled round the circle? (It grew louder as more people joined in; we made a crescendo.)
When we stopped one by one what happened to the sound? (It became quieter and quieter; we made a diminuendo.)

Extension 2

What you will need
- space to sit in a circle
- a selection of small percussion instruments (one per child)

Play *Pass it on* with the instruments. The children can make any sound they choose on their instrument (it does not have to be rhythmical). Apply the same rules as before.

Questions you might ask
Did everyone wait until it was their turn, or did anyone begin playing too soon?
What happened to the sound we made as more instruments were added? (It became louder.)
What did you think of the sound when everyone was playing? (It may have been much too loud for comfort, and some children may have complained.)
How can we play the game without it becoming too loud when everyone is playing? (Each child could find a quiet sound to play.)

Extension 3

Play the game again, this time with a rule that each individual sound is a quiet sound. Does the game still produce a crescendo as everyone joins in, and a diminuendo as the instruments stop one by one? (It should!)

Listen to track 14 Alpha

Questions you might ask
Did the music start loudly or quietly? (Quietly.)
Did the music get louder or quieter? (Louder.)
What made the music louder? (More and more instruments joined in. Some instruments gradually played louder.)

TEMPO

What you need to know about tempo

Music can be performed at varying speeds; we can sing a song slowly or quickly, or at any speed in between. In music the word for speed is tempo (plural, tempi). A guide to tempo is often given at the beginning of written music. The guide may say *play at a walking pace* or *lively and fast*. In classical music, Italian terms, like *allegro* (pronounced a-**le**-gro) meaning quickly, or *adagio* (a-**da**-jeeo) slowly, are often used instead of English words.

Often, music is played at a constant tempo throughout, neither speeding up nor slowing down. In **The little train of the Caipira**, however, the music speeds up as the train accelerates at the beginning of its journey, and slows down as the train approaches its destination. The effect is very exciting. The Italian terms for this are

> *accelerando* (a-**che**-le-**ran**-do) - gradually speed up
> *rallentando* (ral-len-**tan**-do) - gradually slow down

Raghupati Rāghava Rājarām is a traditional South Indian song. In the instrumental version here, the melody of the song is repeated four times, each time at a different tempo. Within each section the speed is constant - it does not get faster or slower. The contrasts of speed between the sections add to the excitement and interest of the music.

Listening links with classroom music

Investigation 1

Think of a song which you all know well. Clap or tap your knees as you sing it at a comfortable speed. Sing another familiar song at the speed which feels comfortable. How do the two speeds compare? Were they different, the same?

Investigation 2

We sing *The Grand Old Duke of York* at a walking speed because it is a march; all try marching round the room or moving your feet, LRLR, as you sing. Now try again at a faster then at a slower speed. Ask the children what it feels like? (Perhaps they have more difficulty stepping in time when it is too slow, or quickly tire when the tempo is too fast.)

Lullabies like *Hush a bye baby* are sung at a slow, rocking tempo. Rock a pretend baby as you all sing the song slowly. Ask the children if it would help the baby go to sleep if they sang the lullaby very quickly. Try it this way. Would it work?

We usually sing *If you're happy and you know it* at a lively tempo. Sing it very slowly - does it sound so happy now?

Listening links with the other tracks

Like *Raghupati Rāghava Rājarām*, *Rippling rhythm* (track 29) has several clear sections, but the music stays at the same tempo throughout. You may like to listen to this effect before the other activities in this section. You will hear a *tik tok tik tok* pattern played on a woodblock in between repeats of the tune; the pattern appears six times altogether:

Listen to track 29 Rippling rhythm

Ask the children, as they listen, to do an action on the *tik tok* pattern whenever they hear it. They could nod their heads from side to side, or tap LRLR quietly on their knees.

Questions you might ask
Was the tik tok pattern always played at the same speed, or was it sometimes played faster, or slower? (It was played at the same speed throughout the music.)

The little train of the Caipira

Composer: Heitor Villa Lobos (born in Rio de Janeiro in 1897, died 1959). Villa Lobos began to teach himself how to compose when his mother stopped his music lessons. As a young man he travelled Brazil listening to and collecting traditional folk music. Many of his compositions include the exciting rhythms and sounds of this music which he loved. He often travelled by train and in *The little train of the Caipira* (pronounced Kye-**pee**-ra) he describes the thrill of taking a steam train journey in the Brazilian countryside.

Villa Lobos uses a large orchestra and many Latin American percussion instruments to create a sound picture of the train journey. The children will be able to hear:

- a reco reco (rray-koo rray-koo, a bamboo scraper), a gourd rattle, a metal shaker, a ratchet and tambourine, sounding like steam pistons speeding up and slowing down,
- the triangle ringing like a train bell,
- in the second part of the journey, the piano playing very fast patterns, moving up and down, round and round, like the train wheels,
- the woodwind instruments and later the brass instruments blaring like the train whistle.

Activity 1

Get on board

What you will need
- a clear space for the children to stand in a circle
- a clear-sounding instrument, e.g. a cowbell and beater

The aim of this movement game is to give the children the feeling of moving at a constant speed.

Stand the children in a circle and explain that you are the train driver. You are going to tap a constant pulse on the cowbell and step on the spot in time to it (**track 15/1**). Demonstrate this to the children and ask them to join in:

Add this chant:

Now explain that you are going to step in time round the circle, and choose someone to join the train. That person, when they hear their name, must follow on behind you, stepping in time with you as you continue round the circle:

Everyone now chants 'Ish-rat, Ish-rat', until you choose another child to join the train. Repeat this until the train is as long as you want or until someone observes that the stepping is no longer in time. The waiting children can watch closely for this. Let individual children be the train driver and observe carefully whether they are able to keep steady time.

21

The little train of the Caipira

Extension 1

What you will need (as above)

The aim here is to give the children the feeling of moving at a gradually increasing speed.

Play *Get on board* again. Start the train slowly. As each child joins on, play the cowbell pulse slightly faster (**track 15/2**). How fast can the train move around the room without getting out of control? Ask the waiting children to observe.

Extension 2

What you will need
- a shaker for each child, e.g. rice in a pot with screw lid

In this version of the game the driver invites passengers to 'get on board' by joining in with their instruments. Play a slow, constant pulse on the cowbell. As you call a name, that child will join in, trying to keep the same speed. Give the children practice at this, then, when a few children are playing, gradually increase the speed.

Encourage the children to concentrate on keeping together as the speed gets faster. Slow down towards the end of the game and call 'All change' to stop. Play it again choosing different children. Notice how they respond to changes in the speed, and let individuals take a turn at being the train driver.

Questions you might ask
Did you manage to play together? If not why not? (Perhaps the driver played faster too suddenly.)
What helped you to keep together when you did it well? (Listening and watching closely, a train driver who speeded up gradually, how well we controlled the instruments.)

Can the children keep in time if the driver is hidden and they cannot see the cowbell being tapped?

Listen to track 16 The little train of the Caipira	

Questions you might ask
What do you think the music is describing? (A train journey.)
What do you notice about the speed of the train at the beginning? In the middle? At the end? (It starts slowly, gradually increases speed, makes an emergency stop in the middle, and slows down at the end.)

Activity 2

Click clack train track

What you will need
- the shakers from the previous activity

Teach the children the chant (**track 17**). To begin with, ask them to join in with the words *click clack train track*. Say each verse at a tempo appropriate to the words, and repeat it as many times as you like. When the chant is familiar ask a group of children to play their shakers on the pulse (marked 🚂). Ask another group of children to listen and observe what happens to the voices and instruments as the tempo changes. Are they managing to stay together?

Listen to the beginning and end of track 16

Ask the children to show where the train speeds up and slows down by moving their arms in time.

Questions you might ask
The train takes you on a journey through the mountains and rainforests of Brazil. What do you find exciting in the music? (Speeding up and moving fast.) What other sounds can you hear? (Train whistle, rainforest, wind, etc.)

Leav - ing the sta - tion, click clack train track,

Ac - ce -le - ra - tion, click clack train track.

Steep hill, down we go, click clack train track,

Ac - ce -le -ran - do, click clack train track.

Forest dark, wind blowing, click clack train track.

Full power to keep going, click clack train track.

Climbing up, getting slow, click clack train track,

Ral - len - tan - do, click clack train track.

Stopping at the sta - tion, click clack train track,

Des - ti - na - tion, click clack train track.

The little train of the Caipira

Extension

What you will need
- untuned percussion instruments for playing the pulse
- a large collection of sound-makers and classroom instruments
- two long sheets of paper and colouring pens
- a cassette player with a recording microphone

Divide the children into two groups. Discuss train journeys the children have taken in town, city or countryside, or talk about fantasy journeys they would like to take. What might they see from the windows? What sounds might be heard?

Group 1 will play the pulse, starting slowly, speeding up the tempo and slowing down at the end. You or a competent child will be the train driver and lead the rest of this group by conducting with actions or playing a cowbell.

Group 2 will provide the sound effects - perhaps the train has a bell or a whistle; it may go past a factory or across a bridge over a river; the wind may be blowing. When the children in this group have chosen their sounds, listen to them one by one and together decide where to draw them on a large draft map of the journey.

When everyone has contributed, use this map as a score of the music. Choose a conductor to point to the score as the train travels along the tracks past all the sights and sounds the children have chosen.

Record this version with a cassette player so that the children can listen to the whole piece. Listen carefully to the combinations of sounds and ask the children which sounds they like and whether they should make any changes. (Perhaps some sounds cannot be heard because others are too loud, perhaps sometimes there are too many sounds at once.) Make any necessary adjustments to the map and play the piece again.

When the children are satisfied with their composition they can make a final, colourful version of the score.

Raghupati Rāghava Rājarām

Raghupati Rāghava Rājarām is an instrumental version of the traditional Indian religious chant (*bhajan* - *b'hah-djun*) of the same name. The chant is very well known and popular among Hindus and was a favourite of Mahatma Gandhi, who changed the words to embrace the different religions practised in India. Like many chants of this type, the singers are usually led by a leader who sings the chant line by line, pausing for the others to copy.

The words of the song praise the gods Rama and Sita, who are particularly celebrated at the festival of Diwali, when the traditional tales of the Ramayana are told. In this instrumental version, the melody of the song is repeated four times, each time at a different tempo:

slow	medium	fast	slow

At outdoor religious festivals in South India, congregations not only sing but also respond in movement to the music by swaying and clapping short rhythm patterns. Singing and dancing congregations move in procession from house to house.

The instrumental version is played on these instruments: violin; nadaswaram (nu-**das**-wah-ram) *top right illustration*; mrdangam (mri-dun-gum) and tavil (tah-vil) - drums *right*; vina (vee-nah) *bottom right*; tamboura (tam-boo-rah) - a stringed instrument for playing drones (see page 26).

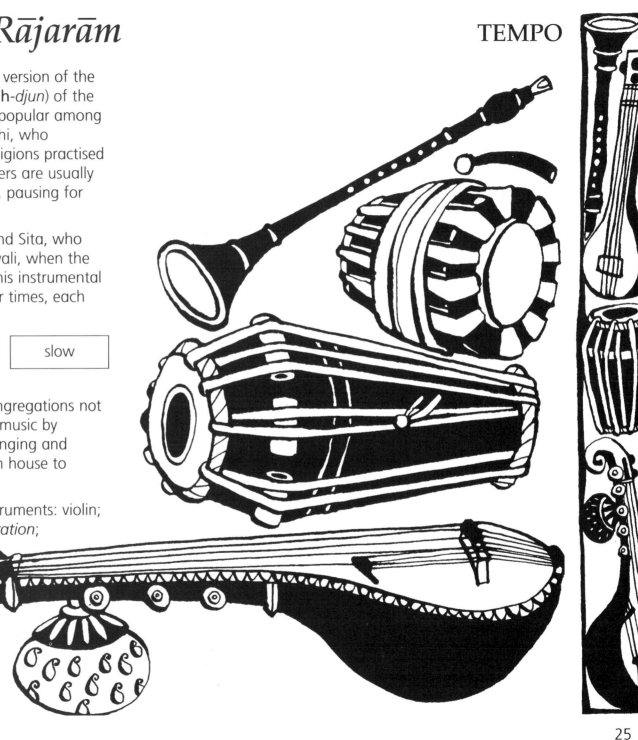

25

Raghupati Rāghava Rājarām

Activity 1

What you will need
- a large space (a hall)

Listen to track 18 Raghupati Rāghava Rājarām

Explain that the music is repeated four times, then play the track to the children one section at a time. Encourage them to respond in movement by swaying from side to side, tilting their heads, stepping on the spot from foot to foot.

slow	medium	fast	slow

Questions you might ask
How did you move in the first section? (Slowly, gently, smoothly.)
What happened to the music in the second section? (It was faster.)
How did your movements change when the music was fastest? (They also became fast.)
What did it feel like when you moved to the fastest music?

Extension 1

What you will need
- at least three sets of wrist or ankle bells made from bells or milk bottle tops threaded onto loops of elastic. If possible have enough sets for all the children

Divide the children into three groups and give at least one child from each group bells to wear on ankles or wrists, then -

---

Play track 18 Raghupati Rāghava Rājarām

Ask the groups to dance in turn to the first three sections of the music. Ask the waiting children to watch and listen. At the end of each section ask the watching children to describe the dancers' movements, the sound of the bells and the speed of the music.

Questions you might ask
When the music was slowest, what did the bells sound like? (Perhaps the dancers were shaking them slowly in time to the music. Some may have shaken them much faster - did this seem to fit with the music? If not, why not?)
As the dancers moved to the fast music, what happened to the sound of the bells? (They were probably shaken faster and sounded more exciting and energetic.)

Extension 2

With the children make up a dance to perform during each verse of *Raghupati Rāghava Rājarām*, matching the movements to the variations in speed: SLOW, MEDIUM, FAST, SLOW. After Activity 2, the children will be able to sing and play along with the dancing.

Raghupati Rāghava Rājarām

Activity 2

Singing Raghupati Rāghava Rājarām

Teach the children the song by singing it to them one line at a time, and pausing for them to copy (**track 19**). When the children are familiar with each line, sing the whole song through as written below (**track 20**).

Raghupati Rāghava Rājarām,
Patīta pāvana Sīta Rām,
Raghupati Rāghava Rājarām,
Patīta pāvana Sīta Rām.
   Sīta Rām Sīta Rām,
   Bhaju pyarē mana Sīta Rām.
   Sīta Rām Sīta Rām,
   Bhaju pyarē mana Sīta Rām.
   Īshwara Allah Tērē Nām
   Sab kō sanmati dē Bhagavān
   Īshwara Allah Tērē Nām
   Sab kō sanmati dē Bhagavān
Raghupati Rāghava Rājarām
Patīta pāvana Sīta Rām
Raghupati Rāghava Rājarām
Patīta pāvana Sīta Rām. (Repeat last line x 3)

Translation: Raghupati Raghava Raja Ram (names of Rama) Rama who is pure, Sita Ram, Repeat in your hearts the names of Sita and Rama, Your names are Christ, Allah. May you endow all (of us) with good intellect.

Listen to track 18 Raghupati Rāghava Rājarām

Questions you might ask
Do you recognise the melody? (It is the same as the song the children have learned. The Raghupati section is repeated in the vocal version.)
How many times did you hear the song melody? (Four times.)
What happened to the music each time you heard it? (The first time it was slow, the second time faster, the third faster still, and the fourth time it was slow again.)

Play the track again

Ask the children to listen carefully to the drumming. The drummers are playing the mrdangam and the tavil (see page 25).

Questions you might ask
What did you notice about the drumming when the music got faster? (It got faster too.)

Extension 1

What you will need
- a pair of drums; one small, one large
- sets of finger cymbals with elastic finger loops

Sing the song together at the four different speeds: slow, medium, fast, slow.

Now give two children the drums and some other children sets of cymbals. Ask them to play along with you as you all sing the song twice - once slow, once fast. Encourage the players to respond to the change in tempo.

Give other children turns at playing along and responding to changes of tempo.

Extension 2

What you will need
- three or four tuned instruments with notes G and C (e.g. G and C chime bars, G and C bars on xylophone or glockenspiel, G and C keys on keyboard)

In this activity the children learn to play a drone, which is a continuous sound made by playing the same notes over and over again. Drones are a common feature of Indian music.

Listen to track 20

The singer is accompanying herself by playing a drone on the tamboura.

Questions you might ask
How many instruments can you hear? (Two - finger cymbals and tamboura)
Do the sounds of the tamboura change or do they keep repeating? (They keep repeating.)

Choose a small group of children to play a G and C drone on the tuned instruments. They should try to make a gentle, continuous sound between them. Encourage them to find their own ways of doing this.

Here are some ideas:

- use two beaters to play a continuous slow roll on the G and C chime bars -

G	C	G	C
L	R	L	R

- choose a setting on the keyboard which makes long sounds, and keep repeating G and C.

As this group plays ask the rest of the children to sing the song together.

Extension 3

Use the ideas you have developed in the previous activities to make a complete performance of the music with groups of singers, instrumentalists and dancers.

TIMBRE

What you need to know about timbre

Every sound has its own unique quality - this is timbre (pronounced **taam**-br).

Even though two sounds may be equally high or low, and may last the same length of time, we can discriminate between them if their timbres are different.

Everyone's voice has a timbre of its own. Children familiar with the game 'Squeak, piggy, squeak' know this well. There are clear differences in timbre between the sounds produced by the wooden bars of a xylophone and the metal bars of a glockenspiel.

Within one instrument there can be a range of timbres, often affected by the way the instrument is played - a drum played with a beater sounds different from the same drum played with the hands; the string of a violin when it is played with the bow sounds very different from the same string plucked with the fingertip.

In **Aquarium** the children will hear the sparkling sounds of a small glockenspiel, a piano, and bowed strings. In vivid contrast with this, are the timbres of the xylophone and plucked strings in **Fossils.**

It is very hard to describe the timbre of a sound, and it is also a very subjective matter. The children may offer very different descriptions from your own or from those suggested in the following activities. Theirs will often be very ingenious. Try to see what lies behind the child's description. Often there are no rights or wrongs. Music is often said to be a language - timbre is part of the vocabulary.

Listening links with classroom music

Investigation 1
Choose a well-known song e.g. *This old man*. Ask the children to sing it in a variety of ways:
- like a lullaby to get a baby to sleep;
- as if they were feeling angry/happy/sad/bored;
- as a pop song;
- as if they were performing in assembly.

Discuss with the children how they have changed their voices and ask them to describe their different timbres, e.g. smooth, gruff, sharp, cool, spiky.

Investigation 2
Collect together story and picture books which use sounds in the text; there are many examples - animal sounds, weather sounds, traffic sounds, traditional tales such as *The Billy Goats Gruff* or *The Three Bears*. Use these as a stimulus for the children to explore different timbres using their own voices and classroom instruments. The aim is to discover musical sounds which appropriately match the quality of the sound they represent, for example a child might choose a zzzzzz with the voice for a buzzing bee, a shaker to match the hiss of a snake, a scraper for the croak of a frog. The children may surprise you with some of their choices, as they will not be so restricted by preconceived ideas. Encourage them to say why they have made a particular choice as they will often have a valid reason which may not be immediately apparent.

Investigation 3
Ask pairs of children to find two percussion or junk instruments with contrasting timbres. Encourage the children to explore different ways of playing the instruments. Will the timbres

always contrast or can the children discover ways to produce similar timbres?

Now ask the children to find two instruments with similar timbres and explore ways of playing these. Will this pair always make similar sounds or can the children devise ways to make contrasting timbres?

Listening links with the other tracks

In Texture (page 39), the children explore combinations of sounds when they sing and play *Punchinello*. Different textures are heard when the sounds of a banjo, spoons, paper and comb, saucepan lid, mouth organ, and bass drum are heard singly and together. But each sound also has a timbre of its own. Ask the children to think about the range of sounds they can make with their mouths and voices, e.g. clicking with their tongues, singing 'shshsh', popping lips together, humming, and so on. How many different vocal timbres can the children discover? Sing *Punchinello* like this and add the children's ideas:

Chorus All:

Look who comes here, Punchinello, little fellow.
Look who comes here, Punchinello, little man.
What can you play, Punchinello, little fellow?
What can you play, Punchinello, little man?

Verse Solo:

I can sing sh sh sh,
Sh sh sh, sh sh sh,
I can sing sh sh sh,
Sh sh sh sh sh.

All repeat verse, then sing chorus again

Verse Solo:

I can laugh, ha ha ha,
Ha ha ha, ha ha ha ...

All repeat verse, then sing chorus again

Continue making up your own verses. The song can be heard on **tracks 27** and **28**.

Listen to track 29 Rippling rhythm

Direct the children's attention to the woodblock *tik toks* which they will hear combined with a long sliding sound on the violin (there is a plan of the music on page 42).

The difference in timbre between the woodblock and violin is striking. Can they find another pair of sounds which are also very different in timbre? (Piano and water bubbles.)

smooth • rough • hard • ringing • sparkling • shiny

Aquarium

Composer: Camille Saint-Saëns (born Paris, 1835-1921).
Aquarium is one of the pieces from *Carnival of the animals*
which Saint-Saëns composed in 1886 to amuse his friends.
Although he would not allow the whole work to be published
during his lifetime in case it damaged his reputation as a
serious composer, it has since become a favourite with
children.

For his musical description of an aquarium, Saint-Saëns
chooses instruments for the distinctive timbres they produce:

- he uses the piano for the rippling sounds which can be
  played on its highest notes;
- he uses the sparkling sounds of the glockenspiel's metal
  bars to conjure up images of tiny, shiny, colourful fish;
- the violins play very high, thin, watery sounds.

Activity 1

Detective

What you will need
- space for the children to sit in a circle
- a collection of sound-makers (one for each child if possible):
rattles, squeakers, whistles, metal washers, off-cuts of wood,
plastic tubs, and classroom percussion instruments

In this game the detective tries to identify a sound-maker by its
distinctive timbre. Sit the children in a circle, each with a
sound-maker on the floor in front of them. One by one round
the circle, each child will make a sound while everyone else
listens carefully.

Questions you might ask
*Were any of the sounds the same or nearly the same? (If any
were, play and compare them again.)*

Repeat the game, but this time say that each sound should be
different, so perhaps some children will need to think of a
different way to use their sound-maker.

Blindfold the detective. Turn the detective gently round in the
centre of the circle. Silently point to one child in the circle to
make a noise with their sound-maker. Turn the detective round
again while everyone chants:

Detective, detective, what did you hear?

The detective then removes the scarf and points to the
instrument he or she thinks was played. That sound-maker is
played and the detective decides whether the answer was
right. If the answer was wrong the detective can point to
another sound-maker. If after three goes the detective is still
wrong, play the original sound again, so that everyone gets
another chance to hear and remember it.

Return to this game often so that everyone has a turn to be
the detective. The game can also be played by the children
themselves in smaller groups.

Activity 2

Rainy day music

What you will need
- a sheet of paper and a colouring pen for each child

The children use sound words for the rain to make up a piece of rainy day music for voices. You may like to use the rain sounds on **track 21** to give the children a starting point.

Ask the children to suggest sounds or sound words for the rain. Collect these together and let each child choose one of them. Ask each child to make their sound or sound word into a simple picture of the type of rain it describes, e.g.

Combine all the pictures into one large rainy day collage. Mount it where everyone can see it so that it can be used as the score for the children's music-making.

To perform *Rainy day music,* point to individual or groups of pictures. As you point the children will make the appropriate sounds with their voices. Try it in a variety of ways:

- everyone makes the same sounds together following the conductor (choose a child to conduct);
- the children only make the sound of their own picture.

Extend the music-making by choosing body sounds (finger taps, stamps, claps) to add to the vocal sounds or by choosing an instrument to substitute for each vocal sound. Play the piece again with the additions and substitutes.

Aquarium

Listen to track 22 Aquarium

Do not tell the children the title before you listen.

Questions you might ask
Can you describe any of the sounds you heard?
Did you recognise any of the instruments? (Piano, violins, glockenspiel.)
Did the music remind you of anything? What might it have been describing? Why?

Discuss the children's different ideas for what the music might be describing. Encourage them to explain the reasons for their descriptions. Tell the children the title of the piece then listen to it again.

Afterwards, explain that people don't always think of the same things when they listen to music. They might think of something quite different from the composer, who in this case wanted to describe an aquarium.

Discuss with the children what they might see and hear in a large aquarium - water bubbling and splashing, fish darting, weed rippling, etc. Listen to the music again and ask the children to think about these questions as they listen.

Questions you might ask
Which sounds might be describing the fish? (Sparkly, tinkling, small, quick sounds.)
How does the composer try to make watery sounds? (Fast notes played on the piano, high sounds, shiny sounds.)

Fossils

Fossils is another piece from Saint-Saëns' *Carnival of the animals*. It features a famous xylophone solo, often heard on television. The composer includes some witty references to some old, 'fossil', French tunes, including *Ah vous dirai-je, Maman* (see page 60) and *Au clair de la lune*.

Activity 1

Sound cards

What you will need
- enlarged photocopies of the instrument and sound cards opposite. Cut and paste them on to separate pieces of card.

Show the children one of the instrument cards and ask them to make sounds with their voices to match that instrument. There may be several different suggestions from different children so share all the ideas with the class. Repeat with the other five cards.

Now place the cards in any order where the children can see them. Hold up the set of sound cards and say the sound on the first card. Ask the children to decide which instrument card they think the sound belongs to. Put the sound card and instrument card together. Repeat with the other five sounds until the children have matched all six pairs. (They may need to reorganise the pairs during the game if they change their minds about any of them.)

Listen to track 23 Sound cards

Listen to sound 1. Can the children match it to a pair of instrument and sound cards? Repeat with the five remaining sounds.

tingting

che-ka che-ka

drrrram drrrram

tiktok

Ping Ping

Wa-waaa

Activity 2

Fossils in the rock

What you will need
- rough stones or rocks, smooth pebbles and fossils (including an ammonite if possible)

Teach the children this rhythmic chant (**track 24**). Say one line at a time and ask the children to copy you. (The rhythm of the words fits the rhythm of the *Fossils* melody.)

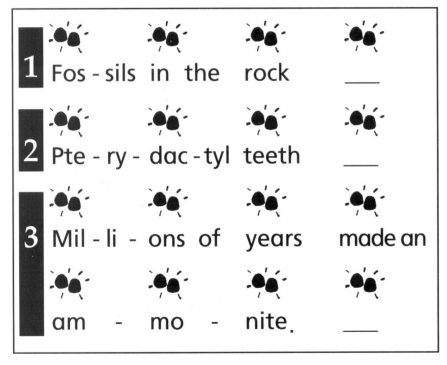

1 Fos - sils in the rock ____

2 Pte - ry - dac - tyl teeth ____

3 Mil - li - ons of years made an

am - mo - nite. ____

When the children know the chant well, ask them to suggest ways of using their voices to say it differently. Try out their ideas: use smooth, gentle voices, or hard, crisp voices, and so

on. Ask three individuals to choose three very different styles and say one line of the chant each, pausing for the others to imitate as closely as possible.

Talk about fossils and how they are formed. Let the children handle the rocks, pebbles and fossils.

Questions you might ask
What do the rocks and pebbles feel like? (Hard, cold, rough, sandy smooth, heavy.)
What do you think pterydactyl teeth would feel like if we were holding them? (bony, sharp, spiky)
What does an ammonite feel like? (Round, ridged, bumpy, light, hard.)

Ask the children to choose a voice sound to use for each line of the chant - 1 rock, 2 teeth, 3 ammonite. When they have chosen three different voice sounds say the chant together again. Change your voices to the style chosen for each line.

Ask one child to accompany the chant, tapping a pulse (marked ⠶) with two rocks or pebbles.

Extension 1

What you will need
- space for three groups of instrumentalists to sit
- a selection of percussion instruments
- two pebbles on which to tap the pulse.

Ask three small groups of children to explore the sound qualities of the instruments, and choose different timbres to play with each line of the chant. They may copy the rhythm of the words or play freely if they prefer.

child 1	*		*	*	*	*	or	*			*	*	*
child 2	*		*	*	*	*			*	*	*	*		**

Fos - sils in the rock   Fos - sils in the rock

Group 1 - Rocks

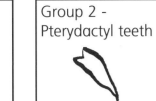

Group 2 - Pterydactyl teeth

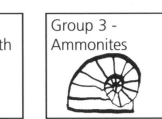

Group 3 - Ammonites

When groups 1-3 have decided which sounds they will use, ask them to play their sounds while the rest of the class listen.

Questions you might ask
What words could we use to describe the sounds made by each group?

Decide how you will put the chant and the sounds together. (An example of how one version corresponding to the plan below may sound is given on **track 25**).

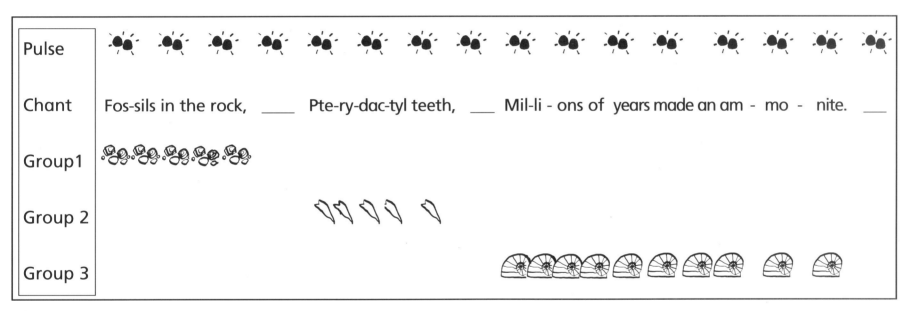

Pulse	
Chant	Fos-sils in the rock, ____ Pte-ry-dac-tyl teeth, ___ Mil-li - ons of years made an am - mo - nite. ___
Group1	
Group 2	
Group 3	

Listen to track 26 Fossils

Questions you might ask
Do you recognise any of the instruments? (Xylophone, plucked strings, clarinet, piano.)
Why do you think the composer chose these sounds?
How are they different or similar to the sounds you chose for your fossil chant?

Extension 2

Combine *Rainy day music* with *Fossils in the rock* to make a piece of music with sections of contrasting timbres. You may choose ternary form, ABA (see page 58), or another structure suggested by the children. Perform it at assembly.

A	B	A
Rainy day	Fossils in the rock	Rainy day

TEXTURE

What you need to know about texture

Sounds can be used singly or in any variety of combinations - this is texture. Texture can be as thin as the sound of a recorder playing alone, or as thick as a large orchestra all playing together.

Often the texture changes within a piece of music, adding to the interest. **Punchinello** is a children's song. In the version on page 40 everyone sings the chorus, 'What can you play?' Next, one person sings the verse solo - on their own - and plays an instrument. Everyone repeats the verse, and in the last verse, everyone sings and plays all the instruments together.

Rippling rhythm is a piece of dance band music, which falls into clear sections, each with a different texture. Whenever the main melody is played by the trumpet many other instruments are also playing, giving this section quite a thick texture. This is interrupted several times by two much thinner textures: a *tik tok* played on a woodblock joined by a low to high slide played on a violin, and a tinkling piano with bubbling watery sounds.

Listening links with classroom music

Choose a well-known song such as *Kum ba ya* and perform it with a variety of musical textures. Here are some ideas to try:

- ask one child to sing a verse as a solo, then repeat it with everyone singing
- add an untuned percussion instrument playing a) on the beat, or b) in the rhythm of the words:

  a) **Kum** ba **ya**, my **Lord, Kum** ba **ya** (play on the **beat**)

  b) <u>Kum</u> <u>ba</u> <u>ya</u>, <u>my</u> <u>Lord</u>, <u>Kum</u> <u>ba</u> <u>ya</u> (play on every <u>syllable</u>)

- change to a different percussion instrument on each new verse
- add one percussion instrument to each verse until several are playing together
- alternate singing each verse with playing the rhythm of the words on percussion instruments.

Listening links with the other tracks

After the activities on **Punchinello** and **Rippling rhythm** you might compare with the children the textures of some of the other pieces. **African drum (track 6)** is a piece of music played by a single instrument. **Divisions on a ground (44)** is a piece for two musicians to play - a duet. The texture is the same throughout - the interwoven sounds of a recorder and an organ. The texture of **Alpha (14)** changes as the piece progresses, and more instruments are added. The first time the melody is played there are very few sounds accompanying it and the mood is relaxed. Then the drum sound is added and later a trumpet and more percussion build up the texture. This gathering complexity has the effect of increasing the excitement and tension of the music. By the end of the piece the texture is very thick and the changes have dramatically altered the mood of the original melody.

Punchinello

This traditional song has been collected and arranged by Alison McMorland, a singer-songwriter, who has spent a lifetime collecting and recording regional variants of folk songs.

Punchinello is a traditional British children's singing game. Like most traditional music it appears in different forms in different places. In one version the children stand in a circle and copy the funny actions of the child in the centre. In this version the children imitate instruments with actions and vocal sounds. The title of the song refers to the Italian character, Pulchinello, who has appeared in popular entertainment throughout many centuries and is the inspiration of Punch and Judy shows.

Activity 1

Sing the Punchinello song

The children learn the song and imitate the instruments. Later on they substitute kitchen instruments and alternate playing them with singing alone and in groups. This will provide a variety of musical textures.

Before you listen to the *Punchinello* track with the children, teach them the song, singing the words opposite. Teach yourself the song first by listening to **track 27**.

Let the children mime playing the instruments and use words to imitate their sounds:

Chorus All (repeat the chorus between each verse):
Look who comes here, Punchinello, little fellow.
Look who comes here, Punchinello, little man.
What can you play, Punchinello, little fellow?
What can you play, Punchinello, little man?

Verse 1 Solo:
I can play on a pair of spoons,
Click click click, click click click,
I can play on a pair of spoons,
Click click click click click.

All repeat:
We all play on a pair of spoons,
Click click click, click click click,
We all play on a pair of spoons.
Click click click click click.

Verse 2 Solo then All repeat:
I can play on a paper and comb
Hoo hoo hoo, hoo hoo hoo ...

Verse 3 Solo then All repeat:
I can play on a saucepan lid,
Crash crash crash, bash bash bash ...

Verse 4 Solo then All repeat:
I can play on a big bass drum,
Boom boom boom, boom boom boom ...

Verse 5 All:
We can play all together ...
(Let each child choose their own instrument to mime and imitate.)

Punchinello

Extension

What you will need
- a collection of kitchen tools: mug and spoon, pair of wooden spoons, pair of yoghurt pots, scrubbing brush and wire sieve, plastic bottle with a little water inside, pair of old pan lids (but nothing sharp!)
- if possible enough multiples of these to supply groups of children with one type of instrument

Choose individual children to take turns to be Punchinello and encourage those children to sing and play by themselves in the solo verses. They might either come out to choose an instrument from the selection or all the children might decide beforehand on the order of the verses.

If you have enough multiples of instruments, divide the children into groups which join in only at the appropriate verse. If there are only enough instruments for the soloists, let the other children all join in together on the repeats of the verses miming the action of playing the instruments and singing the sound words: Here is a sample arrangement:

Chorus All (repeat the chorus after each verse):
Look who comes here, Punchinello, little fellow.
Look who comes here, Punchinello, little man.
What can you play, Punchinello, little fellow?
What can you play, Punchinello, little man?

Verse 1 Solo:
I can play on a mug and spoon,
Tink tink tink, tink tink tink,
I can play on a mug and spoon,
Tink tink tink tink tink.

All repeat:
We all play on a mug and spoon,
Tink tink tink, tink tink tink ...

Verse 2 Solo then all repeat:
I can play on the yoghurt pots,
Clop clop clop, clop clop clop ...

Verse 3 Solo then all repeat:
I can play on a brush and sieve,
Shush shush shush, shush shush shush ...

Verse 4 Solo then all repeat:
I can play on the wooden spoons,
Tap tap tap, tap tap tap ...

Verse 5 All:
We can play all together ...
(let each child choose their own instrument to mime and imitate.)

Rippling rhythm

Composer: Shep Fields (North American).

Shep Fields' Big Band was not thought of as one of the best in 1930's America until *Rippling rhythm* became a hit in 1936 and from then on his players were nicknamed the 'Rippling Rhythms'. It was common for dance band leaders of the time to write light-hearted and humorous pieces, often describing sounds from nature. This piece must have been inspired by streams or rivers as it involved the players in providing authentic sound effects by blowing bubbles in glasses of water!

Activity 1

> **Listen to track 29 Rippling rhythm**
>
> *Questions you might ask*
> *Which words would you use to describe the music? (e.g. funny, happy, bouncy, lively, tinkly, bubbly.)*
> *What was the very first sound you heard? (Bubbles in water.)*
> *How do you think it is being made? (By blowing through a straw into water.)*
>
> **Listen to the beginning of the track again**
>
> *Questions you might ask*
> *Do you recognise any of the instruments playing? (Piano, trumpets, woodblock, violin, accordion.)*
> *What does the violin do? (It plays a long slide, low to high.)*
> *Which instrument can you hear playing with the violin? (The woodblock.)*
> *What sound is the woodblock making? (Tik tok tik tok.)*

Activity 2

Grid score

What you will need
- an enlarged photocopy of the grid score with blanks (page 42)

The aim of this activity is to develop the children's awareness of changes in texture within a piece of music. As they listen to *Rippling rhythm* they will identify the different combinations of sounds (textures).

Show the children the grid score with blanks. Explain that it is a plan which shows some of the sounds they will hear, but that others are missing and need to be drawn in.

> **Listen to track 29 Rippling rhythm**
>
> As you and the children listen, follow the progress of the music on the grid, pointing to each symbol as you hear the appropriate sounds in the music.
>
> *Questions you might ask*
> *Which sounds did we hear when we came to the empty boxes? (Violin and woodblock.)*
> *How many times did we hear this altogether? (Six times.)*

Now ask the children to suggest (or draw for themselves) symbols to represent the missing sounds, e.g.

Rippling rhythm

Grid score with blanks

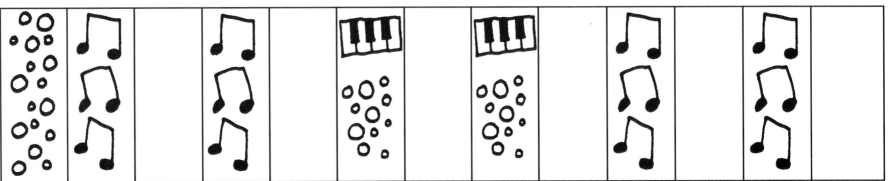

Blank grid

Rippling rhythm cards

Extension

What you will need
- copies of the blank grid and sets of *Rippling rhythm* cards

In pairs, the children sort the cards into the four groups and place them face up in front of them:

Play track 29 Rippling rhythm

As the children listen they will try to place the cards in the boxes on the grid, matching the sounds they hear with the symbols.

They will need to listen to the piece more than once to complete their grid.

Activity 3

Pond life

What you will need
- space for the children to sit in five separate groups
- an enlarged copy of the *Pond life* score (pages 44-45)
- instruments (see below)
- a cassette recorder with recording microphone

Using a pictorial score and *Rippling rhythm* as stimulus the children will explore a number of different musical textures in small groups to make a larger composition called *Pond life*. (An example is given on **track 30**.)

Show the *Pond life* score to the children. Like *Rippling rhythm*, *Pond life* has a succession of different textures.

Divide the children into five groups: Clock, Dragonflies, Frogs, Water bubbles, and Tadpoles. Sit each group in a clear space with the instruments listed below:

	clock: two tone woodblock
	dragonflies: light, high sounding instruments - finger cymbals, bells, triangles
	frog croaks and song: scraper, xylophone, recorder
	bubbles: plastic containers with straws - experiment with different amounts of water
	tadpoles: slides from low to high - glockenspiels, keyboard, metallophones

Rippling rhythm

Pond life continued

Allow each group time to investigate and organise their sounds to make up their own short piece of music.

Clock

Move a pointer across the score from left to right. As the pointer crosses the *tik tok* symbols on the score the children play a steady *tik tok tik tok* on their instruments. Ask them to notice the places when the *tik toks* stop.

Dragonfly dance

Talk about the types of sounds the group can play to describe the dragonflies as they hover or dart over the pond.

Frog song

This group can work out some music for a frog song. Some players might make croaking sounds, and others a lively hopping dance tune.

Water bubbles

Let this group experiment with different amounts of water poured into plastic containers. By listening to different combinations they will choose the effects they like best.

Tadpoles

This group will need practice in holding a beater in a relaxed grip to slide along the bars of glockenspiels or metallophones, from low to high notes (long to short bars.)

Rehearse each group separately, pointing to the score as they play while everyone else listens.

When each group is confident with their own contribution, build up the parts gradually like this:

1. Clock

2. Bubbles plus Dragonflies

3. Frogs plus Tadpoles plus Clock

4. Everyone

Record the results on a cassette player so that everyone can listen to the whole piece when all the parts are combined.

Listen to the ending of track 29 Rippling rhythm

Questions you might ask
How is this different from your ending? (The original ends with two loud sounds played altogether by several instruments; ours ends with the water bubbles.)

Extension

In small groups make up music with picture scores on other themes, e.g. our playground, in the garden, traffic in the street, machines in the home.

PITCH

What you need to know about pitch

Sounds in music can range from low to high - this is what is referred to as pitch. As a general rule the larger the instrument, the lower the pitch. For example, a large drum will make a lower sound than a small drum of a similar type; the larger side of a wooden agogo will produce the lower sound. (*Please note: it is hard to hear the pitch of some instruments such as woodblocks, tambourines or bells.*)

Many instruments produce not one but a whole range of pitches, but the same relationship between size and pitch applies. For example, a double bass, the largest member of the violin family, has long, thick strings and makes a much lower range of sounds than the much smaller violin; a bass recorder makes a much lower range of sounds than the tiny sopranino recorder:

sopranino recorder

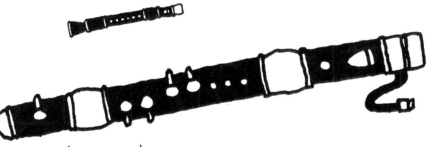

bass recorder

Pythagoras on the line is a piece of music based on the sounds made by telephones. A telephone starts to ring and continues at the same pitch throughout the music, except for one ring with a lower sound. This jump down in pitch gives the impression of a brief 'fault' on the line until the normal ringing tone is restored.

Divisions on a ground is played by the smallest and highest-sounding recorder, the sopranino, while an organ plays a lower-sounding repeating pattern known as a 'ground bass'.

NOTE: talking about pitch with young children can often be confusing as they use the terms higher and lower in relation to volume - 'Turn the radio down. Turn the music up higher'. It is important to be aware of this in the following activities.

Listening links with classroom music

Investigation

Sing the first few words of familiar songs with the children and ask them to show with their hands in the air how the tune moves up and down. They will need to sing each opening several times to discover its shape. (You can hear the following song openings on **track 31**.)

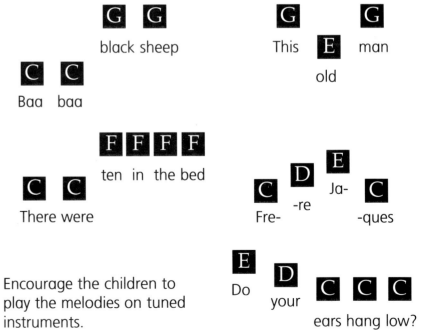

Encourage the children to play the melodies on tuned instruments.

Listening links with the other tracks

After the activities on *Pythagoras* and *Divisions on a ground* -

Listen to track 29 Rippling rhythm

Questions you might ask
When we hear the piano with the bubbles, is it playing high notes or low notes? (High.)
Can you hear what the violin is playing when we hear the tik tok woodblock? (It is sliding up from a low to high pitch.)
How do you think this sound is made on a violin? (The player slides a finger along the string shortening its vibrating length. Perhaps a child who is learning to play the violin, or guitar, would demonstrate this.)

Play the extract several times so that the children are able to identify the sounds. Ask them to count the violin slides - there are six altogether.

Listen to track 32/1 African drum

The drum imitates the rhythms of speech. Speech has rhythm but it also goes up and down in pitch, and the drum imitates this as well. The drummer can produce higher pitches by squeezing the drum to make its skins tighter.

Enlarge the four cards opposite and place them where the children can see them all. Listen to the track again and trace each shape on the card one pattern at a time.

Now listen to track 32/2 Drum quiz

You will hear the patterns played in a different order. Can the children match them with the cards? (3/1/4/2)

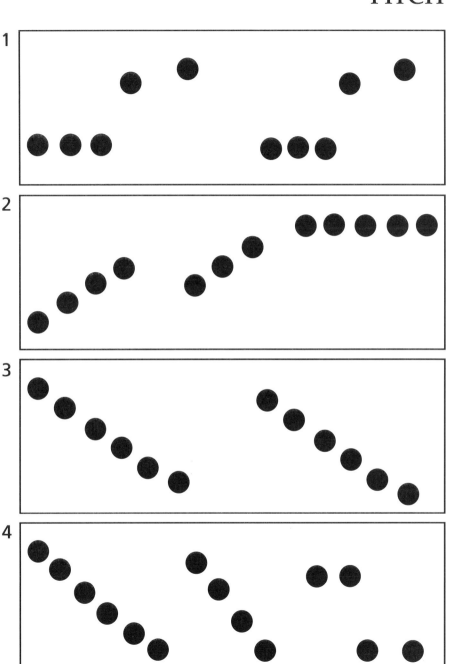

high low • getting higher getting lower • staying the same

Pythagoras on the line

Composer: Simon Jeffes wrote *Pythagoras on the line* for computer in 1993. He says his ideas for composition come from 'everything I hear', in this case the sounds made by telephones.

The Greek mathematician, Pythagoras, was the first to investigate the mathematical principles of musical pitch. This is one of the reasons why Jeffes has chosen him to make this particular telephone call.

Activity 1

Listen to track 33 Pythagoras on the line

The children will recognise the sound of the ringing telephone. Encourage them to use words to describe how the music made them feel. (Was it surprising, strange, funny, calm?)

Talk about telephone sounds the children are familiar with. Mention different types of telephone - dial, button, mobile, call box - and listen together to all the telephone sounds the children can make with their voices.

Giant, mouse and me

What you will need
- enlarged photocopies of the telephone cards opposite

Listen to track 34 Giant, mouse and me

There are three different telephone ringing tones.

Questions you might ask
Which phone made the lowest sound? (The third.)
Which made the highest sound? (The first.)
When you were listening to each of the phones, did you hear the sound go up, or down, or did it stay in the same place all the way through? (It stayed in the same place.)

Listen to track 34 again

Show the children the telephone cards and ask them, as they listen, to decide which sound belongs to the giant's telephone (number 3), the mouse's telephone (number 1), and a phone like theirs (number 2).

Questions you might ask
Why did you choose telephone number 3 for the giant? (It has the lowest-sounding ring. A giant is large and has a low-sounding voice.)
Why did you choose telephone number 1 for the mouse? (It has the highest-sounding ring and a mouse has a high-sounding voice.)
Why did you choose telephone number 2 for your own phone? (It sounds like a 'normal' phone.)

Whose phone?

What you will need
- the enlarged giant, mouse and me telephone cards

The aim of this game is to help the children recognise changes in pitch and be able to use their voices to make high, in-between, and low pitches.

Ask one of the children to choose one card without showing it to the rest of the class, then make a telephone ringing sound with their voice to match the card.

Questions you might ask
Can you tell whether it is the giant's phone, the mouse's, or the child's own phone? (If not, why not? Perhaps we need the other two phone sounds to compare. Perhaps, if it was the giant's, the child needs to make a lower sound, or a higher sound for the mouse so that it is clearer.)

Repeat with the other cards. (Some children may make a very loud sound for the giant, or a very quiet sound for the mouse, but not a different pitch. Help them to differentiate.)

The game can be played in pairs with extra sets of cards so that each child has an opportunity to make low, in-between and high pitches with their voice, and also has a turn at recognising them.

Extension 1

Play *Whose phone?* by making all three sounds one after the other. The soloist chooses which order to make the phones ring. This time the listeners have to compare the three sounds, remember them, and say the order in which they were made.

Activity 2

Ring high ring low

What you will need
- two chime bars; a high-sounding bar and a low-sounding bar (one short, one long)

The aim is to give the children experience of hearing a change in pitch and responding to it in movement.

Play track 35 Ring high ring low

Questions you might ask
What is odd about this phone? (The ring jumps down to a lower pitch.)

Ask the children to stand up. Play the track again and ask the children to sit down when they hear the ring jump down.

Show the children the two chime bars.

Questions you might ask
Which chime bar will make the higher sound? (The shorter bar.)
Which will make the lower sound? (The longer bar.)

Now play a ringing tone on the shorter bar. Jump down to the longer bar after a while. Ask the children to move their hands from up to down as you move from the higher pitch to the lower (**track 36**).

Choose a child to play the ringing tones on the short bar while everyone else stands up. When the ringing tone jumps down in pitch to the long bar, everyone sits down.

Now hide the bars and explain to the children that this time they will need to listen carefully to hear the signal to sit down. Play the game several times as a class, and leave the chime bars in a corner of the classroom where the children can play the game in pairs.

Ringing tone

In this game, pairs of children play with pitch changes using their voices then chime bars. In extension 2, they learn how simple graphic notation can indicate pitch changes.

Choose a pair of children to demonstrate the game. The children will be using their voices to make ringing tones (they should each decide first on the type of ringing tone they want to make). The object is to take turns making their phones ring using a drop in pitch to signal the other person's turn.

The children stand back to back. Child A starts to repeat the ringing tone. When Child B hears the ringing tone jump down to a lower pitch, it is Child B's turn.

The game ends when one child decides to make the unobtainable tone - a continuous sound on one pitch. (The picture opposite and **track 37** demonstrate the game.)

A   brr brr   brr brr

beeeeeee

brr brr

B

beep beep   beep beep   beep beep

beep beep

Extension 1

What you will need
- high and low pairs of chime bars

Play *Ringing tone* with chime bars. This time Child A repeats a ringing tone on the high-sounding bar then jumps down to the low-sounding bar.

When the pitch jumps down, Child B begins their telephone ring and the game continues as before.

To make the unobtainable tone use two beaters on one bar and play alternately LRLRLR very quickly to make a 'roll'. The picture below and **track 38** demonstrate the game.

A

B

L R L R L R

Pythagoras on the line

1

2

3

4

5

6

Extension 2

What you will need
- enlarged photocopies of the ringing tone cards above

The aim of the game is to introduce to the children a simple form of pitch notation. The cards show high and low ringing tones, and an unobtainable tone. The children interpret the patterns, using either voices or instruments.

Show the cards to the children. Discuss the different number of times each telephone rings before the pitch of the ringing tone jumps down. Ask the children to make ringing tones with their voices as you or a child point to each symbol in turn.

Notice whether all the children are able to follow the pattern and make their voices jump down in the correct place. One of the cards has the unobtainable tone. Can the children work out which it is? (Card 6 ends with a continuous tone.) (You can hear how each should sound on **track 39**.)

Extension 3

What you will need
- one set of the six ringing tone cards, and two sets of high and low chime bars for each pair of children playing the game.

The aim is to play *Ringing tone* reading from the cards. One child in each pair shuffles the cards and deals out three each, laying them out face up, in a row.

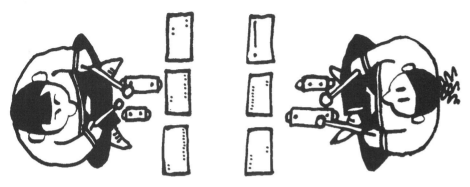

The children take alternate turns to sing or play each of their cards in turn (reading from left to right). As soon as one of the players makes the 'unobtainable' tone (the continuous pitch) the game stops and the cards are dealt again. Take turns to deal. The children may like to make up their own set of cards.

Listen to track 33 Pythagoras on the line

Questions you might ask
What do you notice about the music now? (The ringing tone jumps down in one place.)
What can you hear at the beginning? (Several dialling tones, the engaged signal, then the ringing starts.)

Play the track again and ask the children to show with their fingers when someone is pressing the dialling buttons, and with their hands when they hear the ringing tone jump down. With repeated listenings the children may be able to hear more in the music. (The harp sound moves up and down in waves all the way through - there are other repeating tones which stay on the same pitch.)

Divisions on a ground

Composer: Godfrey Finger (born Moravia, 1660-1730).

Godfrey Finger was a court composer to James II at a time when musicians were particularly interested in the sounds created by different combinations of instruments. They were also developing exciting new musical forms. Divisions were an early type of musical variations (see page 59), in which a simple tune is altered many times in one piece, often showing off the player's skill as the variations become more complicated. In this piece you will hear the tune and its variations played on the smallest and highest-pitched recorder, the sopranino. In contrast an organ plays a repeating low-pitched bass pattern called a 'ground bass'.

Activity 1

Ground bass clock 1

What you will need
- several drums and tambours of different sizes
- a selection of other percussion, e.g. cymbals, woodblocks, triangles, bells - all of different sizes
- an enlarged photocopy of Clock 1 (page 54)

The aim of this activity is to explore the pitches of untuned percussion instruments by investigating and comparing their sounds, then to play the ground bass on pitched percussion.

Divisions on a ground

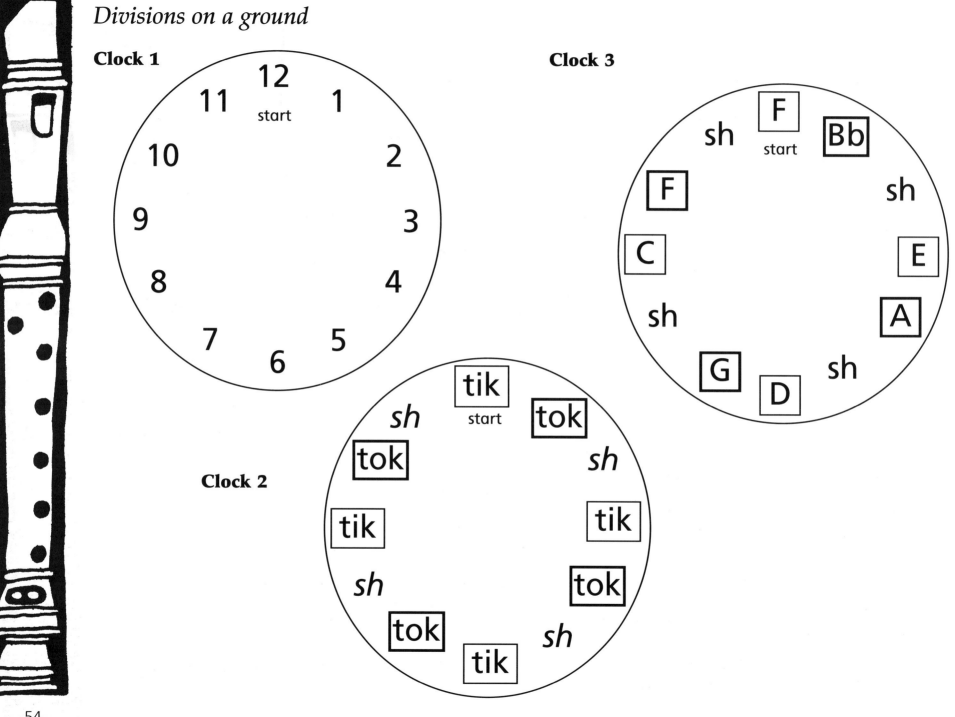

Clock 1

12
start
11   1
10   2
9   3
8   4
7   5
6

Clock 3

sh
F
start
Bb
F
sh
sh
C
E
A
sh
G
D
sh

Clock 2

tik
start
sh
tok
tok
sh
tik
sh
sh
tik
tok
tok
sh
tik

PITCH

Ground bass clock 1 (continued)

Show the enlarged copy of Clock 1 to the children and point to the numbers one by one round the clock face. Ask the children to count out loud with you, starting at 12 and keeping a slow, steady pulse. Count round the clock several times without stopping at 12 o'clock:

12 1 2 3 4 5 6 7 8 9 10 11 12 1 2 ...

Ask a child to choose from the selection of different-sized drums one which will make a low, deep sound (i.e. one of the largest). The class count around the clock again while the drum is tapped on each count.

Now show the children all the percussion instruments you have selected.

Questions you might ask
Are there any other instruments here which you think will make low sounds?
Which instruments do you think will make high sounds?

The children will need time to listen to and compare the sounds of the instruments you have chosen, placing them in two groups HIGH and LOW.

Discard the instruments which seem difficult to fit into either group. There are no right or wrong answers, but check that the children are clear they are not grouping by quiet/loud sounds rather than low/high.

When the children have chosen all the lowest-sounding instruments choose players and a conductor to play and count round the clock together.

Ground bass clock 2

Now the children will learn the rhythm of the ground bass used in *Divisions on a ground*. In the music this repeating rhythm is spread out over a cycle of 12 counts, like the hours on a clock face. Start counting on number 12 so that the strong musical beats fall on numbers 1, 4, 7 and 10. Try counting it like this. (You can hear it on **track 40**.)

12 **1** 2 3 **4** 5 6 **7** 8 9 **10** 11 12 **1** ...

Show the children Clock 2 and explain that this clock has a fault - it only ticks twice in a row then misses a tick! (You can hear this on **track 41**.) Start at 12 again and go round the clock face several times saying:

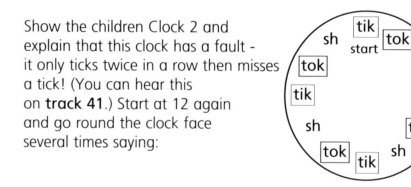

10 11 **tik** **tok** sh **tik** **tok** sh **tik** ...

(12   1   2   3   4   5   6   )

Try again but this time encourage the children to say *sh* in their heads. Ask them to tap their palms each time the clock makes a sound and shake once in the air when the clock is silent. The second tap is louder:

10 11 **tap** **tap** shake tap **tap** shake tap...

(12   1   2   3   4   5   6   )

Divisions on a ground

Ground bass clock 3

What you will need
- prepare the largest tuned percussion instrument you have (bass xylophone or a large metallophone would be best) with these bars:

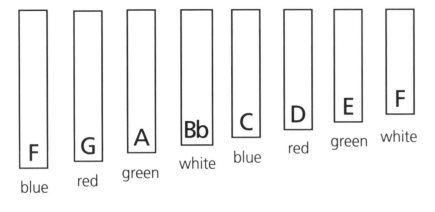

F
blue

G
red

A
green

Bb
white

C
blue

D
red

E
green

F
white

Sticker the bars with the colours shown. Alternatively, sticker the keys of an electronic or piano keyboard with the letters and colours:

Listen to track 42 Ground bass clock 3

This is the bass pattern of *Divisions on a ground*. The children will hear the twelve-count cycle played once, then repeated a number of times.

Show the children the enlarged copy of Clock 3 and as you play the track again, point to the letters on the clock face as they are played:

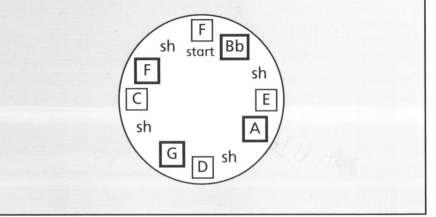

Let individual children practise playing the bass pattern on the prepared instruments:

(F **Bb** sh E **A** sh D **G** sh C **F** sh)
white **white** sh green **green** sh red **red** sh blue **blue** sh

The other children can show with their hands in the air how the pitch moves:

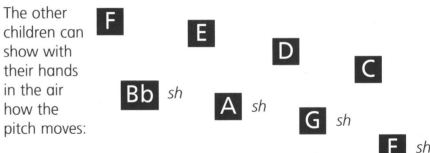

56

Activity 2

Clock improvisation

What you will need
- the high-sounding percussion instruments the children set aside in the first activity, e.g. indian bells, small cymbals, high-sounding chime bars, bells, small rattles, etc
- the low-sounding percussion group from Clock 1
- the Clock 3 group

Arrange the children like this:

This is an improvisation game (**track 43** gives a version of it). The children take turns to make up their own patterns of high sounds while the bass groups keep repeating the ground bass and the count.

Let the low-sounding instruments begin the music by playing once through the ground bass, then signal to the first child in the outer circle to begin. This child freely improvises high sounds while the ground bass is being played and while you or another child count to 12. On twelve, without a break, the first child stops and the second child starts to play. Continue round the circle until everyone has had a turn.

Listen to track 44 Divisions on a ground

The organ plays the very low-sounding ground bass while the high-sounding sopranino recorder plays variations, or divisions, of the melody.

Questions you might ask
How many instruments do you think are playing? (Two.)
Which instrument do you think is playing the high notes?
Do you recognise the sound of the instrument playing the low sounds?
Which words would you choose to describe the organ tune? (Low, repeating, steady, slow.)
Which words describe the recorder music? (High, fast, fancy, light, happy.)
Does the recorder play the same thing all the way through, or does it keep changing. (It changes each time the organ repeats its pattern.)

There is one place where the organ plays a long series of notes which get higher step by step. Play the track again and ask the children to listen carefully. Can they say what happens?

STRUCTURE

What you need to know about structure

Composers use a variety of structures to organise their music. One common structure makes an ABA pattern - the first and last sections (A) are the same or very similar, and the middle section (B) is different. A small-scale example of this is the song *Twinkle twinkle little star*.

Theme and variations is another very common structure. A theme or melody is taken and developed in a succession of different ways: the tune might be changed, or the sounds that go with it, or the rhythm might be altered, and so on. Mozart wrote a set of variations for piano based on the French melody, **Ah, Vous Dirai-je, Maman**, which has the same tune as *Twinkle twinkle little star*.

Listening links with classroom music

Play a copy action game with the children, e.g.

You	clap clap clap	Class	clap clap clap
You	nod nod nod	Class	nod nod nod
You	stamp	Class	stamp
You	wiggle	Class	wiggle

Encourage the children to notice that each action is repeated.

Play another action game: Switch. This time the children do the action with you. When you say 'switch' you all change to a new action. Choose a small number of actions for each round of the game.

At the end of each round ask the children how many different actions there were. Were any of the actions repeated or were they all different?

Choose some well-known action songs and sing them with the children. Ask the children to identify any actions and words which repeat, e.g. in *The Hokey Cokey* there are three sections:

Beginning	Middle	End
You put your right hand in, right hand out, in out, in out, shake it all about.	You do the hokey cokey and you turn around, that's what it's all about.	Oh, the hokey cokey, oh, the hokey cokey, oh, the hokey cokey, knees bend, arms stretch, ra ra ra.

The melody of each section stays the same each time it is sung. The beginning has a different action with each new verse - hand changes to arm, leg, whole self, etc. The middle section and the end are always the same.

Investigate other action games with the children. Can the children recognise different sections and spot where and how they repeat or change? *Heads, shoulders, knees and toes*, *We're going on a bear hunt*, *Wind the bobbin up*, and *The wheels on the bus* are some to explore.

Listening links with the other recordings

AB structure

This, like ABA structure, is very common. There are two sections of contrasting material. The children will already be familiar with this structure because the chorus and verse of a song form an AB structure. **Punchinello** is a chorus and verse song:

A (chorus) Look who comes here, Punchinello little fellow ...

B (verse) I can play on a ....

Mu min xin ge is an instrumental piece with an AB structure of two contrasting sections. Section A is free in rhythm with quiet, slow moving long sounds. Section B has a strong pulse and rapid short sounds which give the piece speed and energy.

Theme and variations

Divisions on a ground is a form of musical variations on a theme, popular in Europe during the 16th and 17th centuries. The divisions were often made up, improvised, by the performer and gave an opportunity for the musician to demonstrate skill. In this piece the recorder plays a short melody which is then repeated several times, each time decorated in a different way (the original music has 25 divisions). The divisions are played over the same bass pattern called a ground, heard here on the organ.

Ragupati Rāghava Rājarām is also a theme with variations. The melody is played four times at varying speeds:

slow   medium   fast   slow

Each time we hear the melody at a faster speed it has the effect of increasing the excitement, relaxing at the end when the original speed returns.

Alpha is yet another example of a theme with variations. Although the melody is not decorated or played at different speeds , Vangelis adds more sounds as the music progresses. The first time we hear the melody it is quiet and the mood is very calm. As the texture of sounds grows, so does the volume and by the end of the piece the atmosphere of the same melody has been transformed.

Other structures

The little train of the Caipira describes a train journey in music. This piece has three parts which match the scene the composer wants to paint:

- **the beginning** of the journey as the train starts to move off and gather speed
- **the middle** with the sights and sounds of the trip over the Caipira mountains
- **the end** as the train puts on its brakes and draws to a halt in the station.

Rippling rhythm has a more complex structure, which is nevertheless very clear to hear. The piece is made up of many short sections. A low to high slide on the violin, accompanied by a woodblock pulse signals the beginning of each new section; the melody is repeated several times throughout the piece. Ask the children to recognise and count the repeating patterns as they listen. You will find a graphic score of the structure on page 42

Fossils has a similar structure: the xylophone plays a lively melody twice, then stops playing while the piano and strings play different material. The xylophone returns, this time followed by some well-known French tunes played by the clarinet, ending with the xylophone. A plan of this structure might look like this:

A (A repeat)	B	A (A repeat)	C	A (A repeat)
xylophone	strings	xylophone	strings	xylophone
	piano		clarinet	

beginning middle end • repetition • contrast

Ah, vous dirai-je, Maman

Composer: Wolfgang Amadeus Mozart, born Salzburg (1756-91).

The song we know as *Twinkle twinkle little star* was originally a French nursery rhyme which Mozart would have sung and played when he was a child. By the age of five he was already a skilled keyboard player and had begun to make up his own music. This was surely one of the pieces which would have delighted audiences of the royal courts across Europe when Mozart and his sister were taken by their father on concert tours to demonstrate their musical skills.

Activity 1

ABA structure: Twinkle twinkle little star

Sing the song with the children encouraging them to join in making the hand signs as shown (**track 45**).

Questions you might ask
When did we do this hand sign?
(At the beginning and at the end.)

When did we do this hand sign?
(In the middle.)

What order did the
hand signs come in?

What did you notice about the tune each time we did this hand sign?
(It was the same.)

Was the tune the same or different when we did this hand sign? (Different.)

Extension 1

When the children are familiar with the hand signs, let individual children use them to conduct the song.

A	Twinkle twinkle little star, how I wonder what you are	
B	Up above the world so high, like a diamond in the sky	
A	Twinkle twinkle little star, how I wonder what you are.	

60

Extension 2

What you will need
- enlarged photocopies of the star and diamond cards above

Show them to the children. Discuss the order they should go in to match the order of the hand signs and the tune.

Extension 3

Sing *Twinkle twinkle little star* again. You or a child conduct the singing using hand signs or cards. Change the order of the hand signs to BAB or ABB etc. By doing this you can check that all the children are matching the tune to the signs.

Listen to track 46 Theme of Ah, vous dirai-je, Maman

Questions you might ask
What do you notice about the tune? (It is the same as Twinkle Twinkle.)
What instrument is being played? (Piano.)

Listen to the extract again. Ask three children to hold up the stars and diamonds cards at the appropriate times.
The rest of the group can make the hand signs.

Ah, vous dirai-je, Maman

Activity 2

ABA sandwiches

Listen to track 47

There are three examples of ABA structure (musical sandwiches). Listen to each separately and ask the children what was different about the middle of each sandwich.

1 quiet   2 slow   3 drum
   loud   **fast**   **bell**
   quiet   slow   drum

Ask the children to make their own musical sandwiches. Can they think of other contrasts to make?

Stars and diamonds

What you will need
- a variety of metal sound makers: bells, milk bottle top shakers, tambourines, a small glockenspiel, indian bells, spoons, triangles, chime bars, etc

With the children, sort out a set of star sounds and a set of diamond sounds. For example, the stars set may make sparkling, shimmery sounds; the diamonds hard-edged, bright sounds. Divide the children into a star group (A), and a diamond group (B). Explain that they are going to make up some music with the same pattern as the song: A B A

Discuss how to play - perhaps in the rhythm of the words, or playing freely. Talk about volume - should the music be loud or quiet? Choose a conductor to lead the groups either with hand signs or cards.

Listen to track 48 ABA quiz

There are three short pieces to listen to. Which of the three have an ABA pattern? (1 and 3.)

Activity 3

Variations on Twinkle twinkle little star

What you will need
- enlarged photocopies of these code cards:

A   1 1 5 5 6 6 5 - 4 4 3 3 2 2 1 -

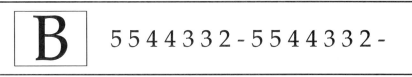

B   5 5 4 4 3 3 2 - 5 5 4 4 3 3 2 -

- two sets of tuned percussion prepared like this:

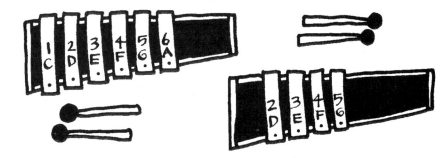

Sticker the bars with the numbers and letter names.

Ask individual children to play the A or B part of the number code on the tuned percussion. Do they recognise the tune? (*Twinkle twinkle little star*.)

When the children are confident with this, ask how they can make up some variations. For example they could play the number code

- backwards;
- in a different order;
- in a different rhythm - some notes longer, some shorter;
- at different volumes - some notes loud, others quiet.

Ask individuals or pairs to perform their variations for the rest of the class. Can the listeners identify how the melody has been changed?

Listen to track 49 Ah, vous dirai-je, Maman

Questions you might ask
How has Mozart changed the melody? (Var II - the rhythm is changed in the first two sections; extra notes are added to the third section. Var III - A sections: melody played in groups of notes; B section: melody played on low-sounding notes.)

Extension

Combine the music the children composed in stars and diamonds with the melody and variations they have made up in this exercise. Draw a pictorial score of the piece. Here is an example of the theme. Can the children notate their variations? (**Track 50** gives a version of the score below.)

63

Index of terms, composers and instruments

Acknowledgements

The following have kindly granted their permission for the use of copyright recordings included on the accompanying recording:

ARC Music Productions International Ltd for **Mu min xin ge** performed by Li He (Chinese Bamboo flute) ARC EUCD 1155 © 1991 ARC;

BMG Records (UK) Ltd for **Alpha** from Albedo.39 by Vangelis CD ND74208 © 1976 BMG Records (UK) and by kind permission of EMI Music Publishing Ltd;

EMI Records Ltd for **Aquarium** and **Fossils** from *Carnival of the Animals* by Saint Saëns performed by the Scottish National Orchestra conducted by Alexander Gibson CD CfP 4086 © 1975 EMI Records Ltd; and for **March past of the kitchen utensils** from *The Wasps* by Vaughan Williams, performed by the London Philharmonic Orchestra conducted by Sir Adrian Boult, CDM 7 64020 2 © 1987 EMI Records Ltd;

Music of the World for **Raghupati Rāghava Rājarām** (trad.) performed by Vadya Lahari. Raghupati Rāghava Rājarām is released on the recording 'Vadya Lahari' © 1992 Music of the World Ltd, USA. The piece is performed by Vadya Lahari, A. Kanyakumari, violin, Mannargudi A. Easwaran, mrdangam, Kumari N. Vijayalakshmi, vina, Mambalam K.S. Siva, nadaswaram and Yarpanam K. Ganesa Pillai, tavil;

Countdown Media for **The little train of the Caipira** from Bachianas Brasilerias No. 2 by Villa Lobos, performed by the London Symphony Orchestra conducted by Sir Eugene Goossens, Everest CD EVC 9007 © Countdown Media/Madacy Entertainment Inc;

Shapiro Bernstein & Co Ltd for **Rippling rhythm** (Gioe, Fields) © by Shapiro Bernstein & Co Ltd, London W1V 5TZ;

Tangent Records Ltd for **Punchinello** performed by Alison McMorland and The Excelsior Band © Tangent Records Ltd BBX 504;

Zopf Limited and The Penguin Cafe Orchestra for **Pythagoras on the line** by Simon Jeffes from the CD Union Cafe on the Zopf label no. 5184102, © 1993, published by Editions Penguin Cafe Limited;

Other recordings are copyright A&C Black: tracks 6, 7 and 32 performed by Sonny Akpan (voice and dondo) of EXTEK Percussion; tracks 19 and 20 performed by Pushkala Gopal (voice, tamboura and finger cymbals); track 27 performed by Rosamund Chadwick (voice); track 44 performed by Caroline Kershaw (sopranino recorder) and Timothy Roberts (organ); tracks 46 and 49 performed by Timothy Roberts (piano); remaining tracks devised and performed by Helen MacGregor and Stephen Chadwick.